英文小說解讀攻略

奇幻篇

戴逸群 —— 主編

簡嘉妤 —— 編著

Ian Fletcher —— 審閱

三民書局

國家圖書館出版品預行編目資料

英文小說解讀攻略：奇幻篇／戴逸群主編；簡嘉妤編
著. －－二版一刷. －－臺北市：三民，2020
　　面；　公分. －－（閱讀成癮）

4712780666814
1. 英語 2. 讀本

英文小說解讀攻略：奇幻篇

主　　　編	戴逸群
編 著 者	簡嘉妤
審　　　閱	Ian Fletcher
責任編輯	林雅淯
美術編輯	陳奕臻
封面繪圖	Steph Pai

發 行 人	劉振強
出 版 者	三民書局股份有限公司
地　　　址	臺北市復興北路 386 號 (復北門市) 臺北市重慶南路一段 61 號 (重南門市)
電　　　話	(02)25006600
網　　　址	三民網路書店 https://www.sanmin.com.tw

出版日期	初版一刷 2020 年 5 月 二版一刷 2020 年 8 月
書籍編號	S870490
	4712780666814

— 序 —

　　新課綱強調以「學生」為中心的教與學，注重學生的學習動機與熱情。而英文科首重語言溝通、互動的功能性，培養學生「自主學習」與「終身學習」的能力與習慣。小說「解讀攻略」就是因應新課綱的精神，在「英文小說中毒團隊」的努力下孕育而生。

　　一系列的「解讀攻略」旨在引導學生能透過原文小說的閱讀學習獨立思考，運用所學的知識與技能解決問題；此外也藉由廣泛閱讀進行跨文化反思，提升社會參與並培養國際觀。

　　「英文小說中毒團隊」由普高技高英文老師與大學教授組成，嚴選出主題多樣豐富、適合英文學習的原文小說。我們從文本延伸，設計多元有趣的閱讀素養活動，培養學生從讀懂文本到表達所思的英文能力。團隊秉持著改變臺灣英文教育的使命感，期許我們的努力能為臺灣的英文教育注入一股活水，翻轉大家對英文學習的想像！

戴逸群

Contents

Picture Credits

All pictures in this publication are authorized for use by Shutterstock.

Word Power

1. mysterious *adj.* 神祕的
2. drill *n.* (電) 鑽；鑽機
3. beefy *adj.* 壯碩的
4. tantrum *n.* 耍脾氣
5. peculiar *adj.* 奇怪的
6. cloak *n.* 斗篷
7. stiffly *adv.* 僵硬地
8. rumor *n.* 謠言
9. flatter *v.* 奉承
10. noble *adj.* 高尚的

Reading Comprehension

(　　) 1. Which of the following can be used to describe Mr. Dursley?
- (A) Mysterious / severe-looking / kind / a professor of Hogwarts.
- (B) Normal / beefy / unimaginative / the director of Grunnings.
- (C) Strange / muscular / timid / the Keeper of the Keys.
- (D) Tall / courageous / wise / the Headmaster of Hogwarts.

(　　) 2. Which of the following was **NOT** one of the things that was out of the ordinary on the dull, gray Tuesday?
- (A) Dudley was throwing a tantrum.
- (B) A cat was reading a map.
- (C) A lot of people on the streets were wearing cloaks.
- (D) There had been hundreds of owls flying since sunrise.

(　　) 3. How did Hagrid deliver Harry to Privet Drive?
- (A) By taking the Hogwarts Express.
- (B) By riding a broomstick.
- (C) By running like lightning.
- (D) By riding a flying motorcycle.

1. The Dursley's greatest fear is people discovering that they are related to the Potters. What do you think the Potters might be like from the way the Dursleys act?

_____

_____

_____

_____

_____

_____

2. Describe Professor McGonagall. What does she look like? What do you think the author is telling us about her personality?

_____

_____

_____

_____

_____

_____

3. Though we often say, "Don't judge a book by its cover," we can tell quite a bit about a person from observing their appearance, clothing, way of speaking and behavior. Try to find examples of how the author describes three characters in chapter 1.

_____

_____

_____

_____

_____

_____

Come up with the headlines that the residents of Privet Drive would find in the newspaper on the next day. (Please base the headlines on the strange things that have happened in the town.)

By Mea quam

Eam sale illum cassae eu, mei ei sint constituto descruisse, ea quod movet legendos usu. Erat zril viderer ea sea, te ciita indicabit laboramus sed, eu ius volutpatat commune vertercen vix.

The Old News Paper

ERAT ZRIL DISSENTIET EU EAM SALUTAT

LOREM IPSUM · DOLOR SIT AMET, APPELLANTUR EA EQUIDEM NOMINATI PETENTIUM · CU HABEO GRAECE CONSTITUAM CUM · CONCLUSIONEMQUE PER CU, TE PRO TAMQUAM

OLD WORLD NEWS

STRANGE PHENOMENA ALL AROUND: IS IT THE APOCALYPSE?

2

Pages 18-30

Word Power

1. rap *v.* 敲
2. groan *v.* (不高興的) 哼聲
3. punching bag *n.* 出氣包
4. wig *n.* 假髮
5. cabbage *n.* 高麗菜

6. revolting *adj.* 令人反感的
7. reptile *n.* 爬蟲類
8. snooze *v.* 小睡
9. vanish *v.* 消失
10. forbid *v.* 禁止

Reading Comprehension

(　　) 1. Which glass vanished in the zoo?
    (A) The glass between the visitors and the amphibians.
    (B) The glass between the visitors and the reptiles.
    (C) The glass between the visitors and the mammals.
    (D) The glass between the visitors and the fish.

(　　) 2. Which of the following was **NOT** one of the reasons that Harry could go to the zoo?
    (A) Marge hated Harry, and she wouldn't want to look after him.
    (B) Mrs. Figg broke her leg.
    (C) Dudley and Piers wanted Harry to come along.
    (D) Aunt Petunia's friend was on vacation.

(　　) 3. How many birthday presents did Aunt Petunia promise Dudley in total?
    (A) 39.
    (B) 37.
    (C) 30.
    (D) 41.

Further Discussion

1. The author describes Dudley as "a pig in a wig." Come up with different animals to describe other three characters you've read about so far.

   _____

   _____

   _____

   _____

   _____

   _____

2. What kind of parenting advice would you give Aunt Petunia and Uncle Vernon?

   _____

   _____

   _____

   _____

   _____

   _____

3. What kind of relationship do you think Harry and Dudley have? Use textual evidence to support your idea.

   _____

   _____

   _____

   _____

   _____

   _____

Put the following items (1–15) in their respective categories. Some items may fall in more than one category. Then, answer the following two questions.

Please mark capital **P** for physical bullying, **S** for social bullying, **V** for verbal bullying, and **N** for not considered bullying. The first one has been done for you.

<u> S,V </u> 1. Making fun of someone.

            2. Hitting or punching someone.

            3. Trying to stop someone from joining a group on purpose.

            4. Stealing, demanding, or damaging someone's belongings.

            5. Acting as though someone is not there or ignoring them.

            6. Disagreeing with someone's comment online.

            7. Trying to make others not to be friends with someone.

            8. Saying mean or humiliating things to someone.

            9. Spreading untrue rumors about someone.

            10. Being angry at someone who has taken your things.

            11. Teasing someone about not being good at sports.

            12. Tripping or shoving someone whenever they go past.

            13. Not sharing your things with others.

            14. Mimicking others unkindly.

            15. Using homophobic or racist remarks.

1. What kinds of bullying did Harry go through? Give textual evidence with the correct items (1–15) from above.

2. If someone you knew were bullied, what would you do?

3

Pages 31–45

Word Power

1. crutches *n.* 拐杖
2. emerald *adj.* 翠綠色的
3. tremble *v.* 顫抖
4. faint *v.* 暈倒
5. clutch *v.* 緊抓

6. furious *adj.* 非常生氣的
7. strangled *adj.* 哽咽的
8. stream *v.* 湧
9. shrivel *v.* 萎縮
10. filthy *adj.* 骯髒的

Reading Comprehension

(   ) 1. What did Uncle Vernon do to stop Harry from getting his letter the third time when the letter arrived?
    (A) He hid the letter in the kitchen cabinet.
    (B) He asked the post office to stop delivering the letters.
    (C) He threw the letters out of the window.
    (D) He slept at the foot of the front door.

(   ) 2. Where did Harry and the Dursleys stay for the night before Harry's eleventh birthday?
    (A) A gloomy hotel on the outskirts of the city.
    (B) A shack on a rock out at sea.
    (C) 4 Privet Drive, Little Whinging, Surrey.
    (D) Room 17, Railview Hotel, Cokeworth.

(   ) 3. Why did Dudley have two bedrooms?
    (A) Dudley was too chubby to fit in just one room.
    (B) Dudley often had sleepovers.
    (C) Dudley used the second bedroom as a storage room.
    (D) Dudley kept a pet owl and a snake in the other room.

1. Why did Harry Potter want to read the letter so badly?

_____

_____

_____

_____

_____

_____

2. On page 32, Harry got back at Dudley by saying, "The poor toilet's never had anything as horrible as your head down it—it might be sick." What did he mean? Try to find or think of something like that that doesn't involve curse words.

_____

_____

_____

_____

_____

_____

3. The birthday gifts Harry received from the Dursleys before were all broken or useless. Write about the meaning of giving gifts. What is the best gift you have ever received and why?

_____

_____

_____

_____

_____

_____

Checklist

If you are planning a surprise birthday party for a family member or a friend, what would be on your checklist?

Things to do:

☐ Set up the budget.

☐ Choose a party theme (Halloween, Disney characters).

☐ _____

☐ _____

☐ _____

☐ _____

☐ _____

Items to prepare:

☐ Flowers, scented candles, photos, balloons for decoration.

☐ Plates, cups, utensils, napkins.

☐ _____

☐ _____

4

Pages 46-60

Word Power

1. tangled *adj.* 糾結在一起的
2. demand *v.* 強烈要求
3. kettle *n.* 水壺
4. squashy *adj.* 易壓扁的，軟的
5. bewildered *adj.* 困惑的

6. stammer *v.* 結結巴巴地說
7. rant *v.* 怒罵
8. abnormal *adj.* 反常的
9. codswallop *n.* 胡說八道
10. insult *v.* 侮辱

Reading Comprehension

( ) 1. What did Hagrid do to Uncle Vernon's rifle?
    (A) He made it disappear.
    (B) He bent it into a knot.
    (C) He tossed it into the fire.
    (D) He turned it into rubber.

( ) 2. What did Uncle Vernon and Aunt Petunia tell Harry about his parents' death?
    (A) They told him that his parents died in a car crash.
    (B) They told him that his parents were blown up by a wizard.
    (C) They told him that his parents died of cancer.
    (D) They told him that his parents were set up by others.

( ) 3. What did Hagrid use as a "magic wand"?
    (A) A sausage.
    (B) A kettle.
    (C) An umbrella.
    (D) A boa constrictor.

Further Discussion

1. If you could cast spells on Uncle Vernon and Aunt Petunia, what would you do?

   _____

   _____

   _____

   _____

   _____

   _____

2. If you were to recruit a Keeper of Keys and Grounds at Hogwarts, what would you list as the requirements for this job? What would the job description be?

   _____

   _____

   _____

   _____

   _____

   _____

3. Do you think what Uncle Vernon and Aunt Petunia told Harry about his parents is a white lie? What can be considered a white lie?

   _____

   _____

   _____

   _____

   _____

   _____

Harry's Emotions

Harry's feelings went up and down during this night. Write down how Harry felt during each of the events and fill out the intensity of the emotion. Use different colors to express different emotions.

Events

frightened

BOOM! Somebody was knocking to come in.

Harry received a chocolate birthday cake.

Harry finally had the chance to read his letter.

Harry found out the truth about his parents.

Hagrid added a pigtail to Dudley's bottom.

Intensity

5

Pages 61-87

Word Power

1. alley *n.* 小巷
2. mumble *v.* 咕噥
3. enchantment *n.* 魔法
4. cauldron *n.* 大釜
5. spleen *n.* 脾臟

6. scatter *v.* 撒
7. infernal *adj.* 地獄般的
8. savage *n.* 野蠻人
9. sneer *n.* 譏諷
10. phoenix *n.* 鳳凰

Reading Comprehension

(　) 1. Who was **NOT** at the Leaky Cauldron when Harry went there?
  (A) Doris Crockford.
  (B) Professor Quirrell.
  (C) Dedalus Diggle.
  (D) Griphook.

(　) 2. If Harry had stroked the door of vault seven hundred and thirteen at Gringotts, what would have happened?
  (A) The door would have melted away.
  (B) He would have been sucked through the door.
  (C) A dragon would have blown fire at him.
  (D) He would have been turned into a stone.

(　) 3. What are the characteristics of Harry's wand?
  (A) 13.5 inches. Maple and phoenix feather.
  (B) 7 inches. Willow and unicorn hair.
  (C) 11 inches. Holly and phoenix feather.
  (D) 10.25 inches. Mahogany and dragon heartstring.

Further Discussion

1. Please describe briefly how Harry felt on the day he first visited Diagon Alley.

_____

_____

_____

_____

_____

_____

2. How did Mr. Ollivander react when he saw Harry's scar? Why did he say "curious" when Harry got his wand?

_____

_____

_____

_____

_____

_____

3. People at the Leaky Cauldron and Mr. Ollivander were all honored and overjoyed to see Harry. However, at the end of the day, Harry felt confused. Why?

_____

_____

_____

_____

_____

_____

Pop-up Store in Diagon Alley

Design your own pop-up store in Diagon Alley!

Store Name: _____

Products:

In collaboration with:

What makes your store special?

What would be your advertising slogan?

Draw your pop-up store in as much detail as possible.

6

Pages 88–112

Word Power

1. puncture *n.* 小洞
2. stranded *adj.* 被困住的
3. barrier *n.* 路障；障礙物
4. freckle *n.* 雀斑
5. compartment *n.* 隔間，包廂

6. jerk *v.* 猛推
7. goggle *v.* 瞪大眼看
8. corridor *n.* 走廊
9. pasty *n.* 餡餅
10. rummage *v.* 翻找

Reading Comprehension

( ) 1. Why was Uncle Vernon willing to walk Harry into King's Cross station?
(A) He was afraid to upset Hagrid again.
(B) He wanted to see Harry make a fool of himself.
(C) He wanted to see Hogwarts for himself.
(D) He wanted to give Harry a proper goodbye.

( ) 2. Which of the following is **NOT** a member of the Weasley family?
(A) Charlie.
(B) Bill.
(C) Percy.
(D) Goyle.

( ) 3. Please give directions to Hogwarts after getting off the Hogwarts Express.

(1) Cross a great black lake by boat.	(4) Walk along a steep, narrow path.
(2) Go up a flight of stone steps.	(5) Go through a dark tunnel.
(3) Pass through a curtain of ivy.	

(A) (2) → (3) → (4) → (5) → (1).
(B) (2) → (1) → (5) → (3) → (4).
(C) (4) → (1) → (3) → (5) → (2).
(D) (4) → (3) → (5) → (1) → (2).

Further Discussion

1. Harry and Ron ate Bertie Bott's Every Flavor Beans on the train. List at least ten flavors mentioned in the story and think of five special Taiwanese-style flavors.

_____
_____
_____
_____
_____
_____

2. Why did Ron and Harry become friends instantly? How are they similar or different?

_____
_____
_____
_____
_____
_____

3. Why do you think Harry wasn't so keen on becoming friends with Malfoy?

_____
_____
_____
_____
_____
_____

Famous Witches and Wizards Card

If you were a famous witch or wizard, what would your card look like? Based on the format of Dumbledore's card (from page 102, line 23 to page 103, line 4), please draw a picture and write down your name, your position, and a description of your abilities and achievements.

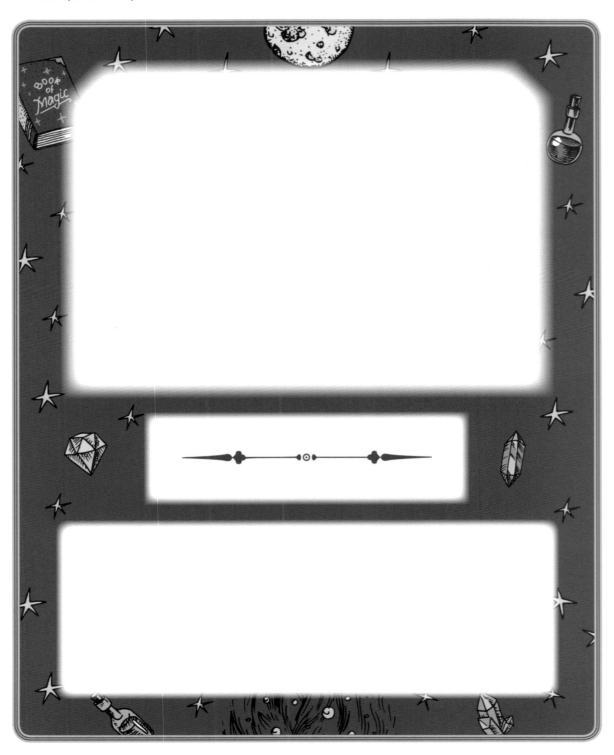

7

Pages 113–130

Word Power

1. stern *adj.* 嚴厲的
2. chamber *n.* 房間
3. triumph *n.* 勝利
4. monk *n.* 修士
5. bewitch *v.* 施魔法

6. troll *n.* 山怪
7. queasy *adj.* 想吐的
8. jam *v.* 把⋯塞入
9. vigorously *adv.* 充滿活力地
10. resident *adj.* 常駐的

( ) 1. Why was Sir Nicholas de Mimsy-Porpington called "Nearly Headless Nick"?
   (A) Because he had no brains at all.
   (B) Because he wasn't beheaded properly.
   (C) Because his head was cut in half.
   (D) Because his head was nearly bitten off by a shark.

( ) 2. During the Sorting Ceremony, the students were called up by Professor McGonagall in _____ order of their _____.
   (A) alphabetical; surnames.
   (B) chronological; last names.
   (C) numerical; registration numbers.
   (D) random; nicknames.

( ) 3. If someone were interested in joining the Quidditch team, which teacher should they contact?
   (A) Professor Snape.
   (B) Mr. Filch.
   (C) Madam Hooch.
   (D) Peeves.

1. Why did Harry want to try on the hat without everybody watching?

_____

_____

_____

_____

_____

_____

2. Why did the Sorting Hat say that Harry Potter was a difficult one to sort? What was the result?

_____

_____

_____

_____

_____

_____

3. Please mark all of the words that rhyme. How many different rhymes are there? Can you come up with 2 other words for each rhyme?

Hogwarts, Hogwarts, Hoggy Warty Hogwarts,	_____
Teach us something please,	_____
Whether we be old and bald,	_____
Or young with scabby knees,	_____
Our heads could do with filling	_____
With some interesting stuff.	_____
For now they're bare and full of air,	_____
Dead flies and bits of fluff,	_____
So teach us things worth knowing,	_____
Bring back what we've forgot,	
Just do your best, we'll do the rest,	
And learn until our brains all rot,	

Hogwarts Houses

Fill in the information of each House and answer the following questions. Some answers will appear in later chapters. When you find them, don't forget to come back and write them down in this form.

	Gryffindor	Hufflepuff	Slytherin	Ravenclaw
Founder	Godric _____	Helga _____	Salazar _____	Rowena _____
Character Traits	_____, daring, chivalrous	_____, hardworking, patient	_____, ambitious, resourceful	_____, intelligent, quick-witted
Animal	Lion	Badger	Snake	Eagle
House Colors	_____, gold	yellow, black	_____, silver	blue, bronze
Head Teacher		Pomona Sprout		Filius Flitwick
Ghost				Grey Lady

1. Which House would the Sorting Hat put you in? Why?

2. Choose a celebrity or famous person to put in each House.

Gryffindor	
Hufflepuff	
Slytherin	
Ravenclaw	

8

Pages 131-142

Word Power

1. rickety *adj.* 搖搖晃晃的
2. patrol *v.* 巡邏
3. ambition *n.* 志向；野心
4. celebrity *n.* 名人
5. stump *v.* 難倒

6. cheek *n.* 無禮的話；厚臉皮
7. collapse *v.* 倒塌
8. drool *v.* 流口水
9. prophet *n.* 預言家
10. grubby *adj.* 髒的

Reading Comprehension

(　) 1. Which would be least likely to happen if you were late and met Peeves the Poltergeist on the way to class?
(A) He would pull rugs from under your feet.
(B) He would throw pieces of chalk at you.
(C) He would sneak up behind you and scare you.
(D) He would point you in the right direction.

(　) 2. If Harry handed in his homework for the following courses, which professors would grade his work?

| Defense Against the Dark Arts / Herbology / Transfiguration / Potions / Charms |

(A) Binns / Flitwick / McGonagall / Snape / Quirrell.
(B) Snape / Sprout / Quirrell / Flitwick / McGonagall.
(C) Quirrell / Sprout / McGonagall / Snape / Flitwick.
(D) Quirrell / Binns / Snape / Sprout / Flitwick.

(　) 3. What might Hermione's notes in Potions class look like?
(A) Monkshood=Wolfsbane=Aconite / Asphodel+Wormwood=Draught of Living Death.
(B) Monkshood+Wolfsbane=Aconite / Bezoar: stone from a goat.
(C) Asphodel+Wormwood= Bezoar / Draught of Living Death=Aconite.
(D) Aconite+Monkshood=Wolfsbane / Asphodel+Wormwood=Bezoar.

1. Why did Harry think that Snape hated him?

_____

_____

_____

_____

_____

_____

2. "Fame clearly isn't everything." What do you think about this sentence?

_____

_____

_____

_____

_____

_____

3. Design a potion of your own. Describe the ingredients included, the effects of the potion, its smell, and its look.

_____

_____

_____

_____

_____

_____

Harry's Social Media Wall

Below are Harry's social media wall and his latest post. Fill out Harry's profile, his friends' names and the comments they would make on Harry's post. Then, draw profile photos for these characters.

Harry Potter

Sep 10 at 17:40

Geez, Potions class was intense! Why does Snape hate me so much?

👍 **Like**　　💬 **Comment**　　↪ **Share**

Harry Potter

My Birthday

July 31st

Check-ins

I go to school at

My friends

My family

Like - Reply

Like - Reply

Like - Reply

Like - Reply

Word Power

1. typical *adj.* 不出所料的
2. prod *v.* 戳
3. scowl *v.* 怒目而視
4. mount *v.* 騎上
5. hobble *v.* 一拐一拐地行走

6. topple *v.* 墜落；跌落
7. burly *adj.* 魁梧的
8. duel *n.* 對決
9. squint *v.* 瞇著眼看
10. lurk *v.* 潛伏；躲藏

Reading Comprehension

(　　) 1. Where were Harry and Draco scheduled to have their wizard's duel?
    (A) In the forbidden forest.
    (B) In the dungeons.
    (C) In Gryffindor Tower.
    (D) In the trophy room.

(　　) 2. Why did Hermione keep following Harry and Ron at midnight?
    (A) She wanted to help Harry defeat Malfoy in the midnight duel.
    (B) The Fat Lady had wandered off and she couldn't get back to her bedroom.
    (C) She wanted to take them to Professor McGonagall and teach them a lesson.
    (D) She was curious about what was hidden in the forbidden corridor.

(　　) 3. What did Harry, Ron, Hermione, and Neville see inside the forbidden corridor?
    (A) A monster with no nose.
    (B) A three-headed pig.
    (C) A three-headed dog.
    (D) Filch's cat, Mrs. Norris.

1. Why do you think Malfoy decided to throw away the Remembrall instead of wanting Harry to chase after him?

_____

_____

_____

_____

_____

_____

2. After the Remembrall incident, what trick did Malfoy play on Harry? Why did Harry fall for it?

_____

_____

_____

_____

_____

_____

3. How did Professor McGonagall see the flying incident? Did she see this incident as a violation of school rules or a demonstration of Harry's flying skills?

_____

_____

_____

_____

_____

_____

Character Analysis

Let's do a character analysis of Draco Malfoy. Complete the table below to understand more about Malfoy.

Appearance/Sound	Behavior
• pale, pointed face (p. 77)	• jeering at his fellow classmates (p. 137)

Personality Traits	Character's Role
• cold, unpleasant	• acting as a contrast to Harry

Comments about Others	Problem and Solution
• About Hagrid: • About Ron: • About Neville:	• On the Hogwarts Express, Malfoy tried to befriend Harry, but instead he felt offended because Harry chose Ron over him. Malfoy responded by saying nasty things about Harry and his friends and sneered at them. • During the flying lesson,

Pages 163-179

Word Power

1. keen *adj.* 渴望的
2. parcel *n.* 包裹
3. beam *v.* 微笑
4. chortle *v.* 哈哈大笑
5. stomp *v.* 重踩；跺腳
6. identical *adj.* 一模一樣的
7. waft *v.* 飄散
8. hover *v.* 盤旋
9. uproar *n.* 譁然
10. petrified *adj.* 嚇呆的

Reading Comprehension

(　) 1. What were the special circumstances that allowed Harry to have a broomstick of his own?
  (A) Harry was going to be a Seeker on the Quidditch team.
  (B) The broomstick was a prize for standing up for Neville.
  (C) This was a belated birthday gift from Professor Dumbledore.
  (D) Harry was going to take Oliver Wood's place as the captain.

(　) 2. There are _____ players in a Quidditch team: _____ Chasers, _____ Beaters, _____ Keeper, and _____ Seeker.
  (A) 7; 2; 2; 2; 1.
  (B) 6; 2; 2; 1; 1.
  (C) 6; 2; 1; 2; 1.
  (D) 7; 3; 2; 1; 1.

(　) 3. How did Dumbledore silence the students when they heard about the troll?
  (A) With purple firecrackers.
  (B) With a mighty roar.
  (C) By putting out all the candles.
  (D) By casting a spell on the students.

Further Discussion

1. Why did Harry and Ron decide to go and check up on Hermione?

_____

_____

_____

_____

_____

_____

2. How did Harry and Ron defeat the troll?

_____

_____

_____

_____

_____

_____

3. What do you think the grubby little package that needs such heavy protection might be? Why does it need so much protection?

_____

_____

_____

_____

_____

_____

Quidditch Flyer

If you were a Quidditch team captain and had to design a flyer that explained the basics of Quidditch for the newcomers, what would your flyer look like? Please write down information (players, equipment, the role of each position, etc.) about Quidditch or draw a picture to explain it.

Quidditch 101

Pages 180-193

Word Power

1. limp *v.* 跛行
2. mangled *adj.* 絞爛
3. sprint *v.* 衝刺
4. diversion *n.* 使分心的事
5. commentary *n.* 實況報導
6. pelt *v.* 飛向
7. lurch *n.* 突然傾斜
8. dangle *v.* 懸掛
9. jinx *v.* 下咒
10. meddle *v.* 管閒事

Reading Comprehension

( ) 1. How did Hermione help Harry and Ron with their homework?
   (A) She let them copy her homework.
   (B) She read through their homework for them.
   (C) She took notes for them in classes.
   (D) She helped both of them work out a study plan.

( ) 2. Who were the Quidditch captains of Gryffindor and Slytherin?
   (A) Alicia Spinnet; Miles Bletchley.
   (B) George Weasley; Terence Higgs.
   (C) Oliver Wood; Marcus Flint.
   (D) Angelina Johnson; Adrian Pucey.

( ) 3. What did Hermione do when she thought Snape was jinxing Harry's broomstick?
   (A) She attacked Snape's injured leg.
   (B) She confronted Snape and made him break eye contact.
   (C) She set the Quidditch stand on fire.
   (D) She set Snape's robes on fire.

1. Harry learned from *Quidditch Through the Ages* that seekers were normally the smallest and fastest players, and most serious accidents happened to them. Why might that be the case?

_____

_____

_____

_____

_____

_____

2. What happened to Harry's broom during the Quidditch game?

_____

_____

_____

_____

_____

_____

3. What position would you like to play on the Quidditch team? Why?

_____

_____

_____

_____

_____

_____

A Day as a Slytherin Commentator

The commentary below is from the perspective of a Slytherin commentator. Please fill in the blanks or check the correct items.

✧ The **Seeker** / (**captain**) of Slytherin, Marcus Flint, is looking fierce and ready to dominate the game!

✧ Gryffindor in possession. YES! Slytherin has regained possession and is about to send the Quaffle through the . . . ahh, Adrian Pucey was going to score, but he was blocked by a Bludger sent from _____ or _____ Weasley.

✧ Gryffindor scores. No sight of the _____ yet.

✧ _____ dodged the Bludger and . . . Marcus Flint was nearly hit!

✧ Slytherin in possession. Adrian Pucey heading to the hoops . . . .

✧ The Snitch! The Snitch shows up! Our _____ and that Potter boy are diving towards it . . . .

✧ But Harry Potter spins off course.

✧ After Marcus' **skillful positioning** / **obvious foul** , he managed to stop Potter from catching the Snitch.

✧ Okay, a free shot for _____ . **Ten** / **Twenty** points won't help them win the game anyway.

✧ Now we're back in the game. Flint with the Quaffle . . . hit by a Bludger . . . hope he's okay . . . and the mighty captain Flint scores once again!

✧ What's going on? Harry Potter is moving strangely. It seems like he can't control his broom! Is Gryffindor going to lose their **Seeker** / **Chaser** ?

✧ Eww! Gryffindor wins after Potter "_____" the Golden Snitch. He didn't even catch it!

12

Pages 194–214

Word Power

1. drafty *adj.* 冷風吹過的
2. grind *v.* 摩擦
3. disgruntled *adj.* 不悅的
4. brandish *v.* (威脅地) 揮舞
5. whittle *v.* (以木頭) 削製
6. hushed *adj.* 低聲的
7. askew *adj.* 歪斜的
8. luminous *adj.* 發光的
9. prop *v.* 靠在⋯；支撐
10. entrance *v.* 使著迷

Reading Comprehension

(　) 1. Which of the following was **NOT** one of the gifts that Harry received for Christmas?
(A) A green sweater.
(B) An Invisibility Cloak.
(C) A maroon sweater.
(D) A wooden flute.

(　) 2. Which of the following was **NOT** one of the things Harry and Ron did during the holidays?
(A) They played wizard chess.
(B) They came up with ways to get Draco expelled.
(C) They played Quidditch in the snow.
(D) They had a hearty Christmas dinner.

(　) 3. What would you need if you wanted to look in a book from the Restricted Section?
(A) A specially signed note from a teacher.
(B) A specially made potion from Snape.
(C) Permission from Dumbledore.
(D) An application form.

1. How did Harry use the Invisibility Cloak? How would you use it?

_____
_____
_____
_____
_____
_____

2. When Harry saw his family in the Mirror of Erised, he felt a powerful ache, "half joy, half terrible sadness." Why might that be?

_____
_____
_____
_____
_____
_____

3. Dumbledore told Harry that the Mirror of Erised "will give us neither knowledge or truth . . . . It does not do to dwell on dreams and forget to live." What can you learn from these pearls of wisdom?

_____
_____
_____
_____
_____

Journal of the Mirror of Erised

Assume that the Mirror of Erised keeps a journal recording the people that come in front of it. Try and write from its perspective what the following people would see if they visited it.

Erised stra ehru oyt ube cafru oyt on wohsi

Please reverse the inscription carved around the top of the mirror.

_____

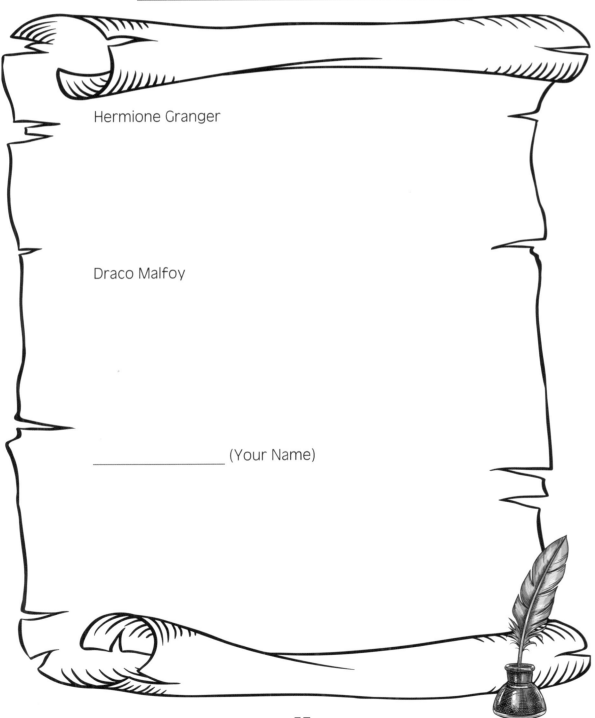

Hermione Granger

Draco Malfoy

_____ (Your Name)

13

Pages 215-227

 Word Power

1. splutter *v.* 語無倫次地說
2. sinister *adj.* 不祥的
3. counter *prefix* 逆，反
4. alchemy *n.* 煉金術
5. biased *adj.* 偏袒的

6. grim *adj.* 無望的；憂愁的
7. somersault *n.* 筋斗
8. brood *v.* 苦思
9. prowl *v.* 潛行
10. strain *v.* 豎起耳朵

Reading Comprehension

( ) 1. How did Harry find out who Nicolas Flamel was?
   (A) Harry found Flamel's book in the Restricted Section.
   (B) Hagrid explained who Flamel was during class.
   (C) Harry remembered he had seen Flamel's name on the Famous Wizard card.
   (D) Flamel appeared in a feature in the *Daily Prophet*.

( ) 2. Which of the following statements is **NOT** true about Nicolas Flamel?
   (A) He is an alchemist.
   (B) He is known to be in possession of the Sorcerer's Stone.
   (C) He can transform any substance into pure silver.
   (D) He is friends with Dumbledore.

( ) 3. How did Harry follow Snape into the forbidden forest?
   (A) He used his Invisibility Cloak.
   (B) He flew on his broom into the forest.
   (C) He followed Snape by foot.
   (D) He used a Transfiguration spell to turn himself into an owl.

1. What did Harry learn about the Quidditch game against Hufflepuff and what did he decide to do? What does his decision say about him?

_____

_____

_____

_____

_____

_____

2. When Harry, Ron, and Hermione learned about Neville's encounter with Draco, they all reacted differently. What do you think their words and actions say about their characters?

_____

_____

_____

_____

_____

_____

3. From this chapter we can see that the Sorcerer's Stone is a prized possession, and that many people want to get their hands on it. Why do you think that is so? Would you like to have it?

_____

_____

_____

_____

_____

_____

Character Word Cloud

Who is your favorite character? Come up with at least ten words related to this character, whether they're about their characteristics, personality, family background, interests, or appearance. Then create a word cloud portraying this character, or you may include a picture, image, or symbol that you think can represent him/her.

My favorite character is:

Words	Textual Evidence

14

Pages 228-241

Word Power

1. nag *v.* 嘮叨
2. shifty *adj.* 可疑的
3. convention *n.* 大會；公約
4. stifling *adj.* 熱得令人窒息
5. fiddle *v.* 無意識地撥弄

6. flushed *adj.* 臉紅的
7. flop *v.* 重重落下
8. furl *v.* 捲起
9. hitch *n.* 小狀況
10. harness *n.* 輓具

Reading Comprehension

( ) 1. How did Hagrid get the dragon egg?

(A) He bought it in a pet store in Diagon Alley.

(B) He won it over a game of cards with a stranger.

(C) Charlie gave it to him as a souvenir from Romania.

(D) He found it abandoned in the forbidden forest.

( ) 2. Where did Draco find the letter Ron wrote to Charlie?

(A) In a book Draco borrowed from Ron.

(B) Draco found it outside Hagrid's hut.

(C) Draco snuck into Gryffindor tower and stole it.

(D) In a book Draco borrowed from the library.

( ) 3. Who caught Harry and Hermione out of their beds in the middle of the night?

(A) Albus Dumbledore.

(B) Draco Malfoy.

(C) Minerva McGonagall.

(D) Argus Filch.

1. What exactly did Harry, Ron and Hermione suspect Snape of? Why?

_____

_____

_____

_____

_____

_____

2. Why were Harry and Ron being friendly toward Professor Quirrell?

_____

_____

_____

_____

_____

_____

3. At first, Hagrid was reluctant to give Norbert away. Later, what changed his mind?

_____

_____

_____

_____

_____

_____

Advertisement for Norbert

Come up with an advertisement that convinces others to adopt Norbert as a pet. Please portray Norbert's characteristics as positive features. You can write and/or draw.

E.g. Does the cold bother you?

Norbert is your solution to chilly winters. You never have to make your own fire again because he BREATHES fire.

15

Word Power

1. alibi *n.* 不在場證明
2. cock-and-bull story *n.* 荒誕的故事
3. thunder *v.* 怒吼
4. rebellion *n.* 叛亂
5. kindle *v.* 激起
6. scud *v.* 掠過
7. quiver *n.* 箭筒
8. hoist *v.* 扛起
9. centaur *n.* 人馬
10. thrash *v.* 劇烈扭動

Reading Comprehension

(　) 1. Which of the following statements is **NOT** true after Harry became the most hated person at school?
　　(A) He offered to resign from the Quidditch team.
　　(B) He spent a lot of time in the library studying for the exams.
　　(C) He decided to poke around and spy on Snape.
　　(D) He resolved to stop meddling and sneaking around.

(　) 2. Why did Neville send up red sparks into the sky?
　　(A) Because he heard something slithering over dead leaves.
　　(B) Because he saw a unicorn lying in the clearing.
　　(C) Because Draco sneaked up behind Neville and scared him.
　　(D) Because a centaur was about to attack Neville and Draco.

(　) 3. What is the value of unicorn blood?
　　(A) It is the Elixir of Life.
　　(B) It can keep you alive no matter how close to death you are.
　　(C) It can be used to make the Draught of Living Death.
　　(D) It can be sprinkled on tombs and bring dead people back to life.

1. Normally students are forbidden to go into the forest. Why do you think the school made an exception allowing them to venture in the forest for detention?

_____

_____

_____

_____

_____

_____

2. Bane and Firenze had different ways of dealing with what they read from the planets. Please describe the differences and elaborate.

_____

_____

_____

_____

_____

_____

3. Who do you think might have given Harry the Invisibility Cloak? The person left a note saying, "Just in case." What might be the case?

_____

_____

_____

_____

_____

_____

Character Log

A lot has happened so far. Please fill out the following form with one quote or one incident from the novel, and then write down this person's physical description or character traits and what he/she lacks. Answers may come from all chapters.

Professor McGonagall

> "Four students out of bed in one night! I've never heard of such a thing before! You, Miss Granger, I thought you had more sense. As for you, Mr. Potter, I thought Gryffindor meant more to you than this." (p. 243)

◆ **Physical Description / Character Traits:**
uptight, strict

◆ **What she lacks:**
the ability to relax

Ron Weasley

◆ **Physical Description / Character Traits:**

◆ **What he lacks:**

Hermione Granger

◆ **Physical Description / Character Traits:**

◆ **What she lacks:**

Draco Malfoy

| | ◆ Physical Description / Character Traits: |
| | ◆ What he lacks: |

Hagrid

| | ◆ Physical Description / Character Traits: |
| | ◆ What he lacks: |

Neville Longbottom

| | ◆ Physical Description / Character Traits: |
| | ◆ What he lacks: |

Pages 262–287

Word Power

1. practical *adj.* 實作的
2. uprising *n.* 起義
3. bask *v.* 曬太陽
4. clamp *v.* 夾緊
5. blurt sth out 脫口而出

6. flare *v.* 張大
7. briskly *adv.* 輕快地
8. hoarse *adj.* 嘶啞的
9. cease *v.* 停止
10. dart *v.* 猛衝

Reading Comprehension

(　) 1. How did Harry get rid of Peeves while they climbed the staircase up to the third floor?
    (A) He sent Mrs. Norris to scare Peeves off.
    (B) He kicked Peeves in the stomach.
    (C) He pretended to be the Bloody Baron.
    (D) He transformed himself into a flight of stairs.

(　) 2. Which of the following was **NOT** included in the practical exams that Harry had?
    (A) Turning a mouse into a snuffbox.
    (B) Making a Forgetfulness potion.
    (C) Making a pineapple tap dance.
    (D) Creating an Anti-Cheating quill.

(　) 3. What did Hermione use to fight the Devil's Snare off?
    (A) Pure water.
    (B) Bluebell flames.
    (C) A wood fire.
    (D) Her bare hands.

1. What skills or talents did Harry, Hermione, and Ron each contribute on their quest for the Stone?

_____

_____

_____

_____

_____

_____

2. Do you agree with what Hermione did to Neville? Why? If not, what would you have done?

_____

_____

_____

_____

_____

_____

3. Harry had already been punished several times for flouting the rules. Why was he still willing to take that risk and go in search of the Stone?

_____

_____

_____

_____

_____

_____

Please write down the obstacles Harry, Hermione, and Ron had to face when they went through the trapdoor and the professors in charge of designing them. (The last obstacle appears in chapter 17.)

No.	Obstacles	Person in Charge
1		
2		
3		
4		
5	Troll	Professor Quirrell
6		
7	The Mirror of Erised	Professor Dumbledore

Now it's your turn to create your own obstacles to protect something as precious and valuable as the Sorcerer's Stone. Get inspiration from the people or things in the magical world, and come up with at least another four obstacles.

Inspiration	Obstacle
Quidditch	Catch a Golden Snitch that is ten times smaller than the normal size.

17

Pages 288–309

Word Power

1. nosy *adj.* 愛管閒事的
2. scurry *v.* 碎步快跑
3. flit *v.* (在腦海或臉上) 閃過
4. edge *v.* 緩慢移動
5. sear *v.* 灼傷

6. hunch *v.* 彎腰；弓起背部
7. knack *n.* 擅長；技巧
8. detest *v.* 厭惡
9. remorse *n.* 悔意
10. sack *v.* 開除

Reading Comprehension

(　　) 1. Who was Ron's hero?
    (A) Rubeus Hagrid.
    (B) Harry Potter.
    (C) Albus Dumbledore.
    (D) Charlie Weasley.

(　　) 2. What is the one thing that Voldemort can't understand?
    (A) Ambition.
    (B) Power.
    (C) Love.
    (D) Greed.

(　　) 3. How many last-minute points did Dumbledore award Gryffindor?
    (A) 170 points.
    (B) 160 points.
    (C) 60 points.
    (D) 50 points.

1. In the last chapter Harry finally met Voldemort. What do we know about him? Why is it that Voldemort is feared by so many?

_____

_____

_____

_____

_____

_____

2. Harry, Hermione, and Ron broke many rules throughout the semester, yet they were never expelled, and they were even awarded points. What can you infer from this?

_____

_____

_____

_____

_____

_____

3. Which is more important, power, or good and evil?

_____

_____

_____

_____

_____

Year-end Report Cards

Imagine that you are one of the teachers at Hogwarts, and you have to write report card comments that are going to be sent to the students and their families. Please choose three other students, and write about both the students' strengths and areas they need to work on.

Student 1

Draco Malfoy

Draco is a kid with lots of potential, and he has been making a lot of progress in Potions class. Madam Hooch has also mentioned that he knows his way around a broomstick. If Draco were to put his brains to his schoolwork, I'm sure his performances would be exceptional. However, he tends to concentrate his energy on being a bully and picking on other students.

Student 2

Student 3

~~~~~~

Student 4

Overall Review

Book Critic

Congratulations on finishing *Harry Potter and the Sorcerer's Stone*. Now imagine you are a renowned book critic, and your fans are waiting for your review of this book.

My Rating:

1. Introduce the book. What are the themes of this book?

_____

_____

_____

_____

_____

_____

2. What is your favorite part of this book?

_____

_____

_____

_____

_____

_____

3. Give a recommendation. (E.g., "If you like . . . , you will love this book" or "I recommend this book to anyone who likes . . . .")

_____

_____

_____

_____

_____

_____

4. Discuss the point(s) of view used in the story. What effect does it have on the story?

_____

_____

_____

_____

_____

_____

5. Choose two to three sentences or scenes from this book that resonate with you and explain your reasons.

_____

_____

_____

_____

_____

_____

英文騎士團長：用繪本、橋梁書和小説
打造孩子英語閱讀素養

作者：戴逸群

★第一本完整蒐羅經典繪本、橋梁書、小説的全
方位英語閱讀教學指南

★閱讀分級系統輕鬆破解，學習英語，從挑對適
合的英語讀物開始

★涵蓋 108 課綱 19 重大議題 X 閱讀素養，透過
素養教案與學習單，英文閱讀輕鬆上手

☞ 本書特色：

◆嚴選經典繪本、橋梁書與青少年小説書單，搭配英語新知學習及反思
問題，增強英語力與思辨分析力。

◆書單涵蓋新課綱 19 重大議題，取材多元，貼近孩子生活課題，培育健
全人格力。

◆導入全美都在使用的藍思閱讀分級系統，精準定位英文閱讀理解力。

◆素養活動教案與學習單結合閱讀策略與閱讀架構圖，深化閱讀素養力。

Answer Key

Lesson 1
Reading Comprehension
1. (B)　2. (A)　3. (D)

Lesson 2
Reading Comprehension
1. (B)　2. (C)　3. (A)

Recognizing Bullying（答案僅供參考）
1. S,V　2. P　3. S　4. P　5. S
6. N　　7. S　8. S, V　9. S, V　10. N
11. V　　12. P　13. N　14. S　15. V

Lesson 3
Reading Comprehension
1. (D)　2. (B)　3. (C)

Lesson 4
Reading Comprehension
1. (B)　2. (A)　3. (C)

Lesson 5
Reading Comprehension
1. (D)　2. (B)　3. (C)

Lesson 6
Reading Comprehension
1. (B)　2. (D)　3. (C)

Lesson 7
Reading Comprehension
1. (B)　2. (A)　3. (C)

Further Discussion
Question 3:
There are 6 different rhymes. 1. please/knees 2. old/bald 3. stuff/fluff 4. bare/air 5. forgot/rot 6. best/rest.

Hogwarts Houses
★ Gryffindor: Gryffindor, brave, scarlet, Minerva McGonagall, Nearly Headless Nick
★ Hufflepuff: Hufflepuff, loyal/just, Fat Friar
★ Slytherin: Slytherin, cunning, green, Severus Snape, Bloody Baron
★ Ravenclaw: Ravenclaw, wise

Lesson 8
Reading Comprehension
1. (D)　2. (C)　3. (A)

Lesson 9
Reading Comprehension
1. (D)　2. (B)　3. (C)

Lesson 10
Reading Comprehension
1. (A)　2. (D)　3. (A)

Lesson 11
Reading Comprehension
1. (B)　2. (C)　3. (D)

A Day as a Slytherin Commentator
Fred, George; Golden Snitch; Harry Potter; Terence Higgs; skillful positioning; Gryffindor, Ten; Seeker; swallows

Lesson 12
Reading Comprehension
1. (C)　2. (C)　3. (A)

Journal of the Mirror of Erised
I show not your face, but your heart's desire.

Lesson 13
Reading Comprehension
1. (C)　2. (C)　3. (B)

Lesson 14

1. (B)   2. (A)   3. (D)

Lesson 15

Reading Comprehension

1. (C)   2. (C)   3. (B)

Lesson 16

Reading Comprehension

1. (C)   2. (D)   3. (B)

Quest for the Stone

1. Fluffy, (Rubeus) Hagrid
2. Devil's Snare, Professor Sprout
3. Winged Keys, Professor Flitwick
4. Chessboard Chamber / Giant Chess
   Set, Professor McGonagall
6. Potions Riddle, Professor Snape

Lesson 17

Reading Comprehension

1. (C)   2. (C)   3. (A)